Roley
and the Woodland Walk

Illustrations by Craig Cameron

EGMONT

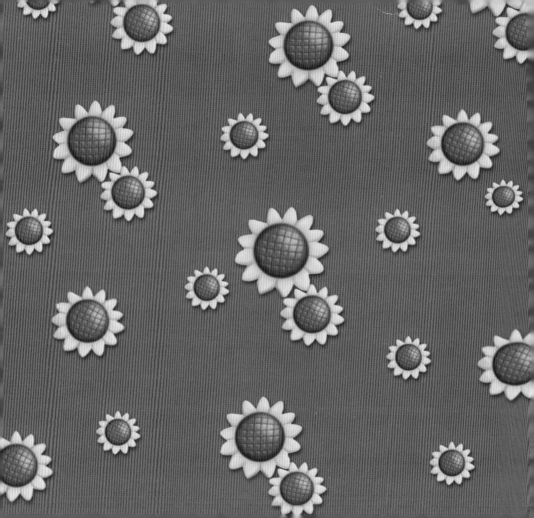

EGMONT

We bring stories to life

First published in Great Britain 2008
This edition published in 2010
by Egmont UK Limited,
239 Kensington High Street, London W8 6SA
Endpapers and introductory illustrations by Craig Cameron.

HiT entertainment

ISBN 978 1 4052 3750 5

1 3 5 7 9 10 8 6 4 2

Printed in Malaysia

When Roley tries to help his woodland friends, they get in the way of Bob and Wendy's work. Until Roley comes up with a brilliant idea . . .

It was a very hot day in Sunflower Valley.

Bob and Wendy were on their way to build workbenches and fit big tools in the workshop.

"We don't need any help, today," said Bob. "So you can all have the day off!"

The machines wanted to keep cool in the shade. So off they all went to the shelter to play 'I Spy'. Except for Roley . . .

Roley set off into Sunflower Valley to look for his friend, Birdie.

"Birdie," called Roley. "It's your friend, Roley. Birdie! Where are you?"

Roley came to a pond in the clearing, but the hot weather had dried up all the water. Next to the pond, he saw Birdie, looking sad. Roley didn't know what was wrong.

"You're not whistling," worried Roley. "Are you too hot?"

Birdie chirped weakly. Roley wondered how he could help. "Maybe I could find you somewhere to keep cool?"

Just then, Birdie's chicks flew on to Roley's cab. As Roley set off to find some shade, a squirrel hopped out of the trees. He was hot, too. "Don't worry," said Roley, kindly. "I'll come back for you."

Roley gave Birdie and her chicks a ride to the storeroom. When they arrived, they flew off his cab and headed for the workshop.

"No, no! Not in there. That's where Bob and Wendy are working," he said, and guided them into the cool storeroom.

Then Roley set off to fetch the squirrel.

Wendy and Bob were building a new cupboard to keep all the tools tidy.

They went to the storeroom to get the first big tool – the saw.

They didn't see Birdie and her chicks nestling under the cover!

Roley zoomed back to the clearing. "It's all right, little squirrel," said Roley. "I've got a lovely place for you out of the sun."

Suddenly, three more squirrels scampered down the trees. "Climb aboard," smiled Roley. Just as he was about to leave, a family of otters dashed out of the bushes. They were hot and thirsty, too.

"Stay here. I'll be right back!" said Roley.

Roley dropped the squirrels off at the storeroom, and then went to fetch the otters.

With the tool cupboard finished, Wendy and Bob wanted to fit the big saw. But when Wendy found the instructions, they were full of holes!

"Oh, no! We can't read this," said Wendy. "Something's been pecking at them!"

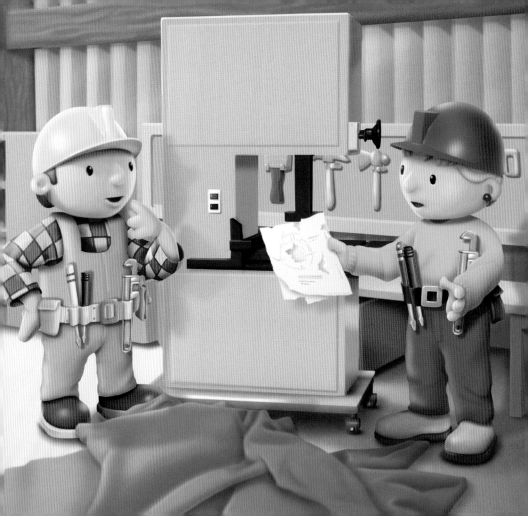

Bob and Wendy couldn't fit the saw without the instructions. They decided to fit the next big tool instead — the drill.

As Wendy pulled off the cover, the squirrels scurried away to hide.

"Look, Wendy!" cried Bob. "These instructions are torn, too."

They were really puzzled now!

Roley brought the otters to the storeroom and looked around inside. "Little squirrel . . . Birdie?" he called. "Are you still in there?"

But they weren't! All the animals were in the workshop.

Roley didn't want Bob to see the animals, so he thought of a plan. "I found Birdie. Um . . . she's not well. She needs our help!" he said, making it up.

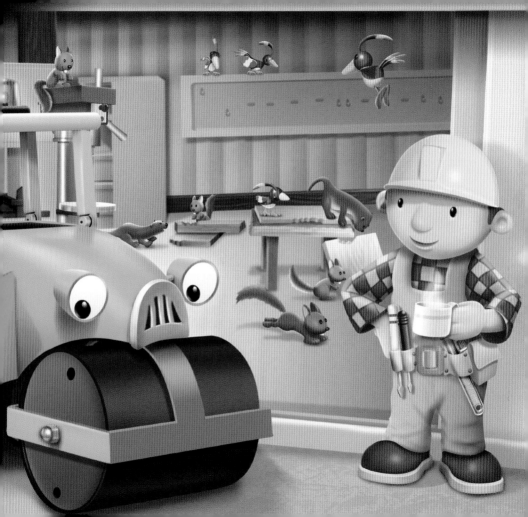

Roley took Bob to the dried-up pond.

"Birdie must be thirsty!" said Bob. "When ponds dry up, birds and animals can't get any water. The best way to help is to put some out for them." Then Bob poured water from his flask. "Now when Birdie comes back, she can have a drink."

Then, Bob and Roley rolled back to the workshop.

Back at the workshop, Wendy had some news for them. "Bob!" she called. "I know why everything was chewed and pecked! The workshop was full of animals! I gave them some water and they've all gone away happy."

Roley felt bad, so he told Bob what had happened. "Don't worry, Roley," said Bob. You were only trying to help."

Suddenly, Roley had a brilliant idea . . .

Roley asked the other machines to help gather up old bits of wood so Bob and Wendy could build a bird table. That way, his woodland friends would have food and water, and he would see them all the time.

The team worked together and soon the bird table was finished. "Rock and roll!" smiled Roley.

And now, whenever the animals get thirsty or hot, they visit Roley's bird table.

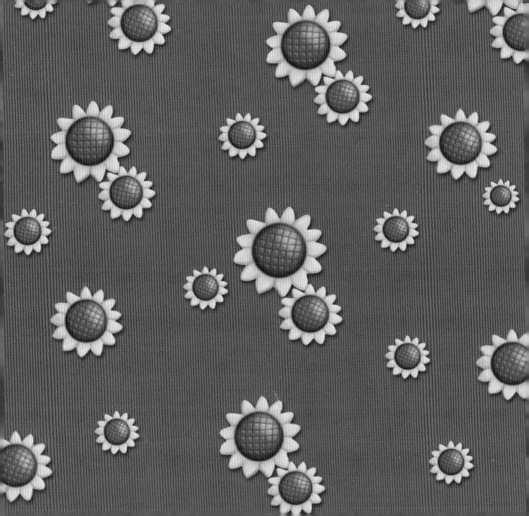

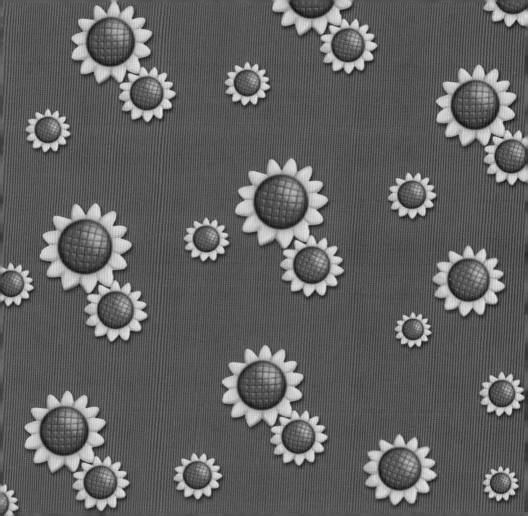